EDGAR and THE TATTLE-TALE HEART

For my mom, who has the kindest heart. —J. A.

For Carol, the original mother bird. —R. S.

First Edition
18 17 16 15 14   5 4 3 2
BabyLit® is a registered trademark of Gibbs Smith, Inc. © 2014, all rights reserved.
BabyLit® brand created by Suzanne Gibbs Taylor for Gibbs Smith.
Text © 2014 Jennifer Adams
Illustrations © 2014 Ron Stucki

Published by
Gibbs Smith
P.O. Box 667
Layton, Utah 84041

1.800.835.4993 orders
www.gibbs-smith.com

Designed and illustrated by Ron Stucki
Printed and bound in China
Gibbs Smith books are printed on either recycled, 100% post-consumer waste, FSC-certified papers or on paper produced from a 100% certified sustainable forest/controlled wood source.

Library of Congress Cataloging-in-Publication Data

Adams, Jennifer, 1970–
  Edgar and the tattle-tale heart : a babylit first steps book / Jennifer Adams ; illustrated by Ron Stucki. — First edition.
       pages cm
  Summary: When Edgar, the mischievous toddler, accidentally breaks a statue while roughhousing with his sister, he must decide whether to tell their mother the truth—and Lenore must decide whether or not to tattle.
  ISBN 978-1-4236-3766-0
[1. Ravens—Fiction. 2. Toddlers—Fiction. 3. Behavior—Fiction. 4. Brothers and sisters—Fiction.] I. Stucki, Ron, illustrator. II. Title.
  PZ7.A2166Ect 2014
  [E]—dc23
                                  2014008889

EDGAR

and THE TATTLE-TALE HEART

BY JENNIFER ADAMS

Illustrated by Ron Stucki

GIBBS SMITH
TO ENRICH AND INSPIRE HUMANKIND

"Edgar, Lenore, I'm going out. I'll be home soon.
Be good while I'm gone."

"EDGAR!"

CRASH!

"Oh, no!"

"Look what you did!
I'm telling mom when she gets home."

"Maybe she won't notice."

"Ed-GAR . . ."

"I'm going to tell!"

"Maybe we can fix it."

"She'll be home soon . . ."

"I'm home!"

"Uh-oh!"

"Mom, Edgar and I were coloring, and then
he started throwing paper airplanes at me,
and then he pushed over the
table, and then . . ."

"Lenore, don't tattle on your brother."

"Edgar, do you have something to tell me?"

"I'm sorry I broke your statue. I didn't mean to."

"Sigh."

"But I made this for you."

"It's okay, Edgar. I love you . . ."

"With all my heart."